*B*I FOUGHT AT *annockburn*

CORBIE

Text by David Ross
Illustrated by Jeffrey Burn

© 2001 Waverley Books Ltd

Published by Waverley Books Ltd
New Lanark, Scotland

ISBN 1 902407 19 9

Printed and bound in Indonesia

I FOUGHT AT
*B*annockburn

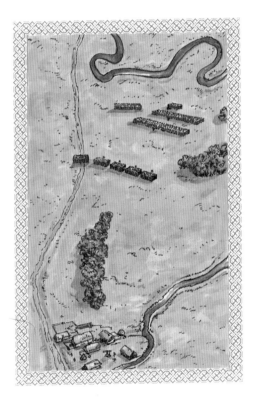

THE FIERY CROSS

I was just coming back from the river with two fine trout when the runner came hurrying into the clachan. He stopped by the well to mop his brow and get his breath back, then called out:

"Tomorrow, at the head of the loch. Clan Donald is gathering."

His eye fell on me.

"Tell them, boy," he said, and set off again. In his hand he bore a rough wooden cross, its ends blackened by burning, with a strip of bloodstained cloth hanging from the cross-bar. I knew what it was. The Fiery Cross! It was the chief's sign to the fighting men of the clan to gather for battle. We had been expecting it for a few days now. It was the middle of June.

"MacDonald has sent round the Fiery Cross," I said, as people began to appear. "We meet at the head of the loch, tomorrow."

"We?"

It was my mother's voice, behind me.

"Yes," I said. "I must go. I have my father's sword."

"You are too young," she said. "Too young. Only – "

"Nearly sixteen," I said.

And I am tall for my age, nearly as big as a grown man. Taller than Fat Calum, my tutor.

My father was the chieftain of the village, cousin to

the chief Angus Og, Lord of Islay. But my father is dead, killed fighting the MacDougalls. When I am properly grown, I will be chieftain here.

"I have already lost my husband for King Robert," said my mother. "Must I lose my son, too?"

"This is not for King Robert," I said. "It is for our country. If the English win at Stirling, everybody knows that will be the end of Scotland."

"Whoever wins at Stirling, many will never come home," said my mother.

"That is the risk of battle," I said, grandly.

"What do you know of battle?" she asked.

"There may not be a battle," said Fat Calum in his smooth voice. "The King is a careful man. He does not like risking everything in one throw of the dice."

"You are supposed to teach this boy the Saxon and Latin languages," said my mother crossly, "not encourage him in wild adventures."

"If he goes, there is nothing else for it. I will have to go too," said Fat Calum. "Someone will have to keep an eye on him."

My mother sighed. "You are as bad as he is," she said. Fat Calum grinned at me. I looked sternly back. Warriors do not grin in that silly way.

THE MUSTER OF CLAN DONALD

Ten men from our village came with me and Fat Calum. We each had a sword, shield, a bag of oatmeal and a cooking girdle. Calum did not own a sword, but had found a big stick. We set off in the early morning and, by midday, I found my gear getting heavy. I was glad when we came near the head of the loch and saw other little groups coming down the hillside. On the flat ground by the shore a great stave had been planted in the ground, with a sheaf of heather bound to it. Beneath this stood the chief. Every little band came up to be greeted by him and report their numbers to his captain.

When he saw me his red eyebrows went up.

"Iain Mor, what are you doing here?"

There was a breathless moment. Everyone looked. I tried to stop my face from going red.

"I have brought my men from Kilmory," I said, hoping desperately that he would not send me home. Angus Og smiled and laid his hand on my shoulder.

"You have done well," he said. "Give your names to the captain and put yourself and your men with Ranald of Arisaig." Ranald was a kinsman of my mother's.

That evening there was a feast of venison, sheep and roast fish. In the long twilight, men moved around,

meeting old friends and exchanging greetings. There was a constant murmur of talk and laughter. Most of us squatted on the ground but the chief and his great men sat at a table in the open air with the chief's own bard, who stood and chanted out a long song of the past glories of the clan and of the chiefs it had had. But he said that none would outshine the deeds of Angus Og, and none outdo the prowess of the warriors before him now. Victory was sure. And if any should fall in the battle to come, then they would be welcomed in the land of heroes beyond the sea, by their own great ancestors. And after that a piper played, and I felt the sound of the war-pipe make my heart beat fast.

We slept in our plaids on the ground that night and on the nights that followed, as we marched through the mountains. I had never been so far away from our village before. I looked with wonder on the mountains and the tumbling rivers. Our land of Alba was so big, so beautiful. In every glen, people ran from their houses to see us go by. Children scampered alongside for a mile or more before turning home. And I saw many a boy of my own age, or older, look with envy at myself.

It was three days before we came down out of the hills and I saw before me a great open plain. The sun, high in the sky, was reflected in the silver loops of a river. Far off to one side, I could just see the glint of the sea. But I was far more interested to look straight ahead, where the smoke rose above the houses of Stirling town. And there, rising on its rock out of the flat ground, was the castle – the last English stronghold in Scotland. Beyond it was open moorland, then rising ground dotted with trees. Somewhere down there was King Robert and the rest of his army, awaiting the arrival of King Edward of England and his knights. Here would be the battle. A murmur went through our whole line as we stood and looked down. Men had been waiting for us – scouts who would lead us to the muster place. From the front, the voice of Angus Og called us on and we set off down the hill, making a wide detour past the town and splashing through the river.

Our meeting point was in the Tor Wood. It was alive with men. I had never seen so many. Most of them had a cross of St Andrew blazoned on their tunics. After we had made our evening meal, our leaders called us to stand. A small group of men came walking up with Angus Og and the other chiefs. Among them was a

man with a red lion on his tunic.

"It's the King," I whispered.

"Silly boy," muttered Fat Calum. "It is a herald, one of the King's messengers. But I know that one – it is the Earl of Moray. And that one, the big dark man, that is the great Sir James Douglas."

And he stood up straight, grasping his stout staff. The little group came towards us. Angus Og was presenting some of the leaders as they went along. And he stopped by me.

"And this is my young kinsman, Iain Mor MacDonald of Kilmory. He has brought ten men to fight."

But Sir James Douglas frowned.

"He is only a boy. It will be men's work here before long. Send him behind the lines."

Angus's face darkened.

"I will do with my men as I think best," he said.

Then a voice broke in. The tall figure of Douglas had concealed another man.

"He shall be by me. Maybe I will need a long-legged boy to carry my orders. If the Lord of Islay will allow it?"

Angus Og bowed low. There was only one man in the world to whom the Lord of Islay would bow. I saw the narrow circlet of gold round the helmet. Suddenly, I realised who this plainly-dressed man was. King Robert was standing in front of me. I knelt down but he motioned me to stand.

"Someone has to be the youngest in the army," he said. "I am pleased that it is the son of your father."

But Fat Calum, having no sword, was sent back, protesting, to join the baggage-men who were in charge of the army's supplies. Whispered rumours seemed to pass through the woodland like the breezes. We could see nothing of the open ground but we soon heard the news.

"The English are here. Their whole army – man, you never saw such numbers."

"We will send them home again!" cried someone. His voice had a ring of false confidence. Ten years ago, the English had held all of Scotland in their grip. It could easily happen again.

"Remember Wallace," someone else called. "Tomorrow we will finish his work."

On the next day we were marshalled into four divisions: the men of Moray and the North, led by the Earl of Moray; the men of Strathclyde, with Sir James Douglas; the men of Galloway, led by Edward Bruce, the King's brother; and ourselves, from the Western Highlands and Islands, together with the men from the King's own home area of Carrick, under the direct command of the King himself.

All day we waited among the trees, which gave us some shelter from the sun and prevented the enemy from counting our numbers. I wished I could see them and longed for the King to send for me, as he had said he would. We were the last in line. Somewhere far ahead, the Moray men were near the castle. All day we wondered what was happening. Then, late in the afternoon, we were called into formation.

"They're coming!"

A few men were out on horseback in front of us. I recognised the King, on a small horse like a Highland garron. Pointing with his battle-axe, he was giving orders to the others, who then moved back to marshal us into a tighter line. It was then we saw the English knight come thundering out of nowhere on his great warhorse. His armour gleamed. His lance was pointing

forward. And he bore straight down upon King Robert. I could not move or cry out. And then, in the blink of an eye, the King had swerved, and even as the knight went galloping past, he rose up in his stirrups and struck him a tremendous blow. The knight fell in a heap from his horse, which cantered away. His shield went spinning through the reedy grass. The King was left looking at the handle of his broken axe. Then my voice came back and so did that of all the Highlanders. A great cheer went up, with cries of "Albannach!"

The King was triumphantly alive – surely it was a sign that fortune was with us. I heard the cheering echo through the woods as the news was passed on through our army.

Our time of waiting was over. Up towards us, like a storm wave, came the glittering sight of the English troops. The King moved off to one side and Angus Og came running to the head of his men.

"Go to him now," he called to me and, reluctantly, I did so. For, like a wave surging in the other direction, the host of the Highlanders was moving out, a torrent of hoarsely shouting men storming onto the attackers. The men of Galloway streamed after them, with Gaelic war-cries.

King Robert was at the edge of the wood, with heralds by him. His eye glanced briefly over me as I appeared then returned to watch the struggle. For the first time I heard the sounds of a battle: the clash of metal, the shouts and screams of men, the high neighing warhorses. Surely these knights would break through! I felt breathless. If they did, I thought, I would be first to put myself in front of King Robert and defend him to the last. But the King was beginning to smile as he watched. And I saw that our men were moving away from us. The English were being forced back. In just a moment, the tight-packed struggle had changed. They were retreating and the Gaels were in full pursuit. The King's face changed again. He spoke rapidly to the heralds and they sped away.

"We must get them back, Iain Mor," he said. "If they chase the English too far, they will be surrounded and that will be the end of them."

"Have we won the battle?" I asked.

He did not mock at my simple-minded question. "The battle has still to happen," he said. "That was only a small part of their army, come to test us out. Tomorrow will be another story."

THE MAN WHO CAME IN THE NIGHT

There had been other fighting that day. Moray and his men had driven back an attempt by a brigade of English cavalry to get past our army and push through to Stirling. On two fronts, our men on foot had defeated heavily armed knights on horseback.

I served the King that evening at the meal in his tent. It was not a great task. He and his captains were eating bread and water, the same as the men outside. Angus Og was there, and Moray, and Sir Andrew Keith, Marischal of Scotland, leader of our small cavalry force. Nor were there only soldiers. I saw a man in a monk's robe – the Chancellor of Scotland, Abbot Bernard of Arbroath. With him was the bearer of a tiny, finely jewelled casket. It was the Brecbennoch, an ancient box, hundreds of years old, containing fragments of the bones of Saint Columba. Tomorrow it would be carried out before the army and shown to us, as one of our country's greatest treasures, a token of our trust in God and a reminder of all that we were fighting for.

There was not much sleep to be had. I bedded down in my plaid in a corner of the King's tent, but woke sometime in the night to see torches flickering and the faces of the King and his captains in eager conversation with a new arrival. As the sense of his words reached

me, I realised that although he was a Scot, he had come over from the English side. The King had been favouring a retreat, unsure whether his army could win against the vastly greater English force. But this man was telling him that the English were poorly led and that they were arguing amongst themselves. They could be beaten.

"We will fight," said the King, and his face was set and sombre. "Let the signal be given at dawn." And he yawned and said, "Dawn is almost here. Let us get some rest while we may."

And I went back to sleep, until the sound of the bagpipes woke me.

We mixed cold brose for our breakfast and drank water. It was still very early. By the King's orders, three brigades – they called them schiltroms, I had learned – moved out. They were the brigades of Edward Bruce, the Earl of Moray and Sir James Douglas. In the open ground, they knelt and said the Lord's Prayer.

There was muttering among us men of the Highlands and Islands. We believed ourselves to be the finest warriors the King possessed. Why then were we held in reserve? Every one of us craved the honour of being first at the enemy. But the King had explained. We were his last and strongest force. He would keep us until he saw clearly where we were most needed.

Afterwards, Fat Calum said, "Actually, he didn't trust the wild Highlanders to stay together in their schiltroms the way the others do, so that the horsemen can't break through."

I gasped when the English cavalry came charging out with their long lances levelled. But they broke against the spears and long-handled axes of Edward Bruce's men. I heard the King cry out, not with triumph but with grief, when the English Earl of Gloucester fell dead from his horse. Later, I learned that Gloucester was his cousin. The King spent a night in church by his body.

Now our other two schiltroms had come face to face with the English and the battle was fully joined. Suddenly out to one side of the English force came the men we feared only a little less than their knights – their archers with the dreaded longbows. Arrows began to shower into the nearest schiltrom.

"Where is a herald?" said the King urgently. Then he saw me. "Ride to the Marischal," he said. "Say to him now is the time for him to do his duty."

I sprang onto one of the horses tethered by us and rode as fast as I could across the front of the trees to where our small cavalry force stood waiting. I gasped my message out to Sir Andrew Keith. He nodded, turned and signed to his men. On smaller and lighter horses than the English knights, they still made a brave sight as they swept down towards the archers. In two minutes, the bowmen were scattered. I turned my horse and galloped back to the King. He was laughing now, his face bright and confident, and as I came up he turned to Angus Og and the other chiefs and shouted to them, "Now, for St Andrew and Scotland!"

At last, the pent-up battle urge of the Highlanders was released. Casting off their plaids, grasping their long swords and shields, they raced forward, shouting their war-cries. Did I say they? I mean we! For I was with them – somewhere near the end of the charging mass of men, still on my sturdy horse, my sword in my hand, yelling like someone stung by a giant wasp.

The English were being forced back, towards the Bannock Burn, the marshy ground beyond it and the broad River Forth.

"On them, on them!" they were shouting by my side. "They fail, they fail!"

A battle is a grisly business. It is only before it, when you are afraid, and after it, when you are glad to be still alive, that you realise this. During it, you have no time to think at all. I still do not know how I obtained the submission of that fine English knight, Sir Marmaduke Tweng. I led him back to the King, his surcoat slashed, his helmet lost and with no more wounds than a black eye and a cut on his cheek.

I do remember the strange charge of the baggage-men. As they saw the English army breaking up and beginning to flee, they came streaming down from the little hill, behind which they had been stationed.

"Lay on, lay on!" they shouted. Among them I had a glimpse of Fat Calum, waving his great cudgel in the air, frantically shouting something, before they swept out of sight.

AFTERWARDS

It is afterwards that you count the cost, in lives lost and broken. Of the ten men of Kilmory, two were buried on the field of battle and one we carried back on a litter. For the dead and those who would never walk again, perhaps it did not much matter whether King Robert or King Edward ruled the Scots. I thought of this a lot as we made our way back through the glens of Alba. But when once again I saw the blue of the western sea and the blue of the islands as we came to the final crest and Kilmory lay below us, I knew, deep within myself, that it did matter. To live in freedom, there is sometimes a price to be paid and those who value their freedom will always be ready to pay it.

NOTE: The Battle of Bannockburn was fought on June 23–24, 1314. You can visit the site of the battle and learn more about what happened and why. Iain Mor ("Big Iain") MacDonald did not really exist, but most of the people mentioned in the story were real people – even Sir Marmaduke Tweng.

Level 4 is ideal for children who are ready to read longer stories with a wider vocabulary and are eager to start reading independently.

Special features:

Clear type

Full, exciting story

Richer, more varied vocabulary

The sun came up over Piggy Island. It was a new day – the day of the Great Fling-Off. The excited birds made their way to the slingshot in time for the start of the competition.

But where were Red and Chuck?

Longer sentences

Detailed illustrations to capture the imagination

"It's no good!" said Red. "We must get the eggs back!"

The other birds were all at the Fling-Off. Only Chuck and Red could save the nest.

"Let's get old helmet-head first!" said Chuck. They set off after Corporal Pig.

Educational Consultant: Geraldine Taylor
Book Banding Consultant: Kate Ruttle

A catalogue record for this book is available from the British Library

This edition published by Ladybird Books Ltd 2014
80 Strand, London, WC2R 0RL
A Penguin Company

001

ISBN: 978-0-72328-906-7

Printed in China

RED AND THE GREAT FLING-OFF

Written by Richard Dungworth
Illustrated by Ilias Arahovitis

Red couldn't sleep. He was too excited. The next day was the day of the Great Fling-Off on Piggy Island. Last year, Chuck had been the winner. "But this year," thought Red, "it's my turn!"

The Fling-Off was the birds' big
competition. They took turns to
fling themselves as far as they
could with the slingshot. The
one who went furthest was the
winner. Red had practised his
fling over and over again.

But what if Chuck has practised more?" thought Red.
Chuck loved competitions. He loved all the training and practising.
He loved to come first, too.

"Perhaps I should do some more training right now," thought Red.

Red made his way quietly to the slingshot. But Chuck had got there first. Just like Red, Chuck was too excited to sleep. Just like Red, he had got up in the night to do some more training.

"Great!" said Chuck. "Now we can train together!"

Red didn't want to help Chuck train. He wanted to be the Fling-Off winner this year. But he couldn't see a way out.

14

"Let's start with speed training!"
said Chuck. "I'll race you to the
top of the mountain. Go!"

The race was very close. Chuck
just made it to the mountain top
first. Red was going so fast, he
went TOO far!

By now, Red was a very angry bird!
"Right!" he said to Chuck. "Let's
see how well you can swim! See that
big rock out there? The first one to
swim there and back is the winner!"

The race was close again. But this time, Red came first. Chuck didn't like that.

"We should test our strength next," he said. So the two birds had another competition.

And then another...

and then another...

21

The sun came up over Piggy Island.
It was a new day – the day of the
Great Fling-Off. The excited birds
made their way to the slingshot in
time for the start of the competition.

But where were Red and Chuck?

Red and Chuck were not far away,
fast asleep. They had been up all
night, training together for the
Fling-Off. And now that the big day
was here at last – they were tired out!

Chuck woke up. "Get up, Red!" he said. "The Fling-Off must be about to start!"

They set off for the slingshot at top speed. But on the way, Red saw something. "Look!" he said quietly. "Over there! Pigs!"

26

Corporal Pig and three other
pigs were sneaking away from the
birds' home. They had something
with them – something that made
Red and Chuck very angry.

"They are sneaking away with
our nest!" said Red.
"And the eggs!" said Chuck.

29

Red and Chuck were about to go after the pigs when they heard a noise. It was the noise that marked the start of the Fling-Off. Chuck and Red looked at one another. They were about to miss the competition.

"It's no good!" said Red. "We must get the eggs back!"

The other birds were all at the Fling-Off. Only Chuck and Red could save the nest.

"Let's get old helmet-head first!" said Chuck. They set off after Corporal Pig.

Corporal Pig made it as far as the mountain. He raced up it as fast as he could. But Chuck and Red were much faster. They soon had the nest back.

"Now for the eggs!" said Red.

The first minion pig thought he would float away. But Red thought not. He could swim much faster than a pig could float! He soon had the first egg back.

"Only two more to go!" he said to Chuck, as he put it in the nest.

Chuck didn't use speed to catch
the next minion pig. He used his
strength – and a very big rock.
Soon there were two eggs back
in the nest.

"Just one more to save!"
said Red with a smile.

Red and Chuck were tired from training all night. But they were not about to let the last pig get away with their egg. Together, they used the last of their speed and strength to catch him.

Red and Chuck were both very glad the nest was full again – but sad they had missed the Fling-Off.

"Perhaps one of us will be the winner next year," said Chuck. "Yes," said Red. "But which one?"

"Don't start that again!"
said Matilda. The other birds
had come racing over to see Red
and Chuck. They were all smiling.
"We saw how you saved the eggs
just now," said Matilda. "And that
makes you both winners!"

How much do you remember about the story of Angry Birds: Red and the Great Fling-Off? Answer these questions and find out!

- What competition does Red want to win?

- Who does Red want to beat?

- Who wins the race to the mountain top?

- Who wins the swim to the rock and back?

- How many eggs do the pigs steal?

- Who tells Red and Chuck they are both winners?